Dreaming Jack

A Lyric Novella

Klaus Merz

Translated from the German by Marc Vincenz

SPUYTEN DUYVIL
New York City

Translation copyright © 2025 Marc Vincenz

Original German-language ©Jakob schläft. Eigentlich ein Roman. Haymon Verlag,
Innsbruck-Wien 1997

Excerpts were published in *The Fortnightly Review*.

Cover design, cover art by t thilleman

swiss arts council

prohelvetia

Printed and bound in the United States of America.

ISBN 978-1-963908-96-1

Library of Congress Control Number: 2025937458

You can see him roving in the evening,

as if walking to a repose

in the light—so the world's mysteries

are captured

impalpably

across all that vastness.

From the poem "Fragment" by Erika Burkart

Cast of Characters

Brother Jack

Uncle Franz

Father

Brother Sol

Mother

Grandmother

Grandfather

Sonja

Marietta

Brettschneider

Mrs. Brettschneider

The Lineman

The Egg Man

and me

ONE

RENZ
Infant

Dust motes rise and fall from the windowsill; behind me, the looming crucifix shrine with its rotting base and its wafer-thin copper roof coated in a blue-green patina. I learned to read from those ten letters seared into the crossbeam.

My older brother died during birth and would actually have been named Jack. But, since there was never an official baptism, my parents compulsively stuck to the official namelessness of their eldest.

Clasping Father's hand, clutching Mother's fingers, and wedged between my grandparents' black winter coats, I repeatedly spelled out that strange description of my brother on the crossbeam:

RENZ
Infant

Gradually the adults wept less frequently at his grave.

Eventually, even visits to the cemetery abated.

That wedding photo of a young couple—the dark clouds of an early pregnancy reflecting in the bride's brilliant eyes—never again perched on the living room credenza.

Begonias were swapped out with pansies, pansies with geraniums. A rosebush lasted longest, until, one day, that rotting crucifix leaned against the woodshed next to the pigsty.

No one in the family knew where else to put it.

A decade later, along with other unwanted personal effects and miscellaneous firewood and clutter—including the workbench and the dented gasoline canister, the wood-splitter and the Harley tires—it likely all passed on to the new owner of the estate.

Shortly thereafter, the estate changed hands a second time and was finally leveled.

In my mind, I stoop once again to avoid smacking my head on the transom of the empty pigsty—just as way back when, in the semidarkness, I smashed open the piggy bank for its shiny fifty-cent pieces.

That dull clang still reverberates.

All those curious coins smoldered in my little clenched fist, sizzled in my tight little palm, and, on the spot, I immediately got what adults meant when they said money couldn't buy happiness.

In order to gloss over my wickedness, I tossed the hand-warmed coins upon the crisp fallen snow and prayed fervently to our Jack, hoping that with heaven's helping hand, he would simply make them dematerialize.

After the snowmelt, the little silvers once again blinked mercilessly up at the sun.

Fearful, I quickly tried to gather them all up.

"Bad boy, Lukas!" Father boomed.

He loomed above, broom in hand on the corrugated tin roof of our flour hopper where a portion of my stash had carelessly been hidden, and stared down disdainfully.

Damn you, Jack! I thought.

As always, plumped up in the sand of our charred birdcage, sat a sparrow.

TWO

You could hear them squawking all the way down to the neighboring village. The tropical birds flapped and flailed around wildly, their wings burning white hot, while Grandfather, garden hose in one hand, axe in the other, simultaneously extinguished and slaughtered.

From the lower village, a siren crept closer.

A cackling, headless kookaburra leaped over the garden fence and ran straight onto the railroad line. A linesman later discovered him lodged between rusty tracks.

The arsonist was never apprehended.

From that moment on, Grandfather simply allowed his fancy feathered friends with their tarnished wings to stay on—the tropical birds whose creaky chants and mantras irritated our neighbors to no end.

Later, one of the two former aviaries served as a sandbox. Here we baked French bread and Bundt cakes, constructed knights' castles, fortresses, and buttresses, and dug ourselves in, toward the very center of the Earth.

On Sunday school days, we let the Great Deluge take her rightful course.

On the south side of the house, the other giant birdcage was converted into a pergola.

And on the daisy-patterned foldout cot that lazed under the mocha-brown camelhair blanket from Sharm El Sheikh (a birthday gift from Uncle Franz), dusty and exhausted from his seasonal nightshifts, Father enjoyed his afternoon snooze.

The inside walls of the extension nook had been painted banana yellow and made me feel I was curled up inside the yolk of an egg. Mother tenderly drew the curtains for Father. Her rambler roses clambered bravely along the sturdy foundation.

On the strip at the end of her garden bed, row upon row of oil flecks had accumulated: a venial untidiness in the shadow of this pristine foliage, a great big heap of pink earplugs.

One afternoon, a shaky, pale Father, camelhair blanket spilling over his shoulders, stumbled into the bakery as if he had just returned from the war.

In his half-sleep he had fallen into an ambush.

The doctors called it epilepsy.

THREE

In the somber light of the aviary, in a low-altitude flight, murmuring silver-grey vampires returned to homebase, and Sonja and I dove deep into our love empire.

We slipped our fingers between each other's naked toes and sniffed them, dazed, until we fell into each other's woozy arms.

Sonja's three impish brothers bravely guarded our love nest while Sonja's father toiled in front of his saddlery, feeding his plucking machine with the same coarse horsehairs that also welled up from beneath his shirt collar.

During summer, he refurbished the sagging mattresses of the entire region—flowery, striped, and polka-dotted—and gifted us the discarded, stained canvas scraps for making our wigwams.

His old mattress straw smoldered on the bonfire.

It kept the horseflies at bay.

During winter months, we rode the worn-out horse saddles of local, industrious families, or crouched like silent natives, drunk on the glue vapors that permeated our dusky encampment.

And, just as they frequently seemed to us during the day, that evening, Sonja's brothers were negligent in their nightly duties.

They nodded off, hunched over their fishing spears, and our parents gently carried us all home to bed.

That path led past a former concrete fishpond that—after those old carp-breeding days (which coincided with Grandfather's birding days)—had now become our fishing pond.

And, when Grandfather's wild carp abandoned their scales and drifted naked on their backs through the concrete fishpond and toward the drain, the water's surface glimmered like a clown's sequined costume.

Then, one stormy night in April, the rivers and streams overflowed
in a great deluge.

Entire houses were submerged.

Potatoes swam willy-nilly out of basement windows.

Falling pine branches tore down overhead power lines, and the end of a wire splashed and crackled in our fishpond.

DO NOT TOUCH!

was emblazoned on the yellow warning sign with the black skull
logo that glared down upon us from every single telephone pole.

We dared not poke the dead fish.

Cloudless summer days and the freshly cleaned fishing pond, with its vitriol-blue shimmer, made the lead-heavy bones of my younger brother seem fleeting and full of light.

He stretched out on the surface like a lazy frog, a black car hose loosely wrapped around his chest, a cork placemat representing a halo lodged carelessly beneath his head.

He became terribly frightened when we rested a BB gun on his stomach and took potshots at the magpies in Mother's lettuce patch.

Every once in a while, the red bellies of wild newts would materialize through the drainpipe and startle him.

Sandpipers, with their long skinny legs, would attack, or a fire salamander might sear his ivory skin.

In our neighborhood, my brother was known as Sol.

Sol didn't scream when the bloated red cat bobbed next to him in the rippling water.

He had drowned it to vent the anger he would never release us from.

And ours toward Sol, too.

And Sonja and I named our birdcage love pergola:

the Orient.

FOUR

"Oh, Franz, thrust your hand in the flames,
that you may burn a guiding light for us!"

Carelessly, while playing his five-fingered fillet knife game, and speeding up to a nervous drumroll, Franz lost his little pinkie finger. Since that time, he preferred setting his 'busted hand,' as he called it, alight.

He doused his hand in gasoline, then lit up.

We were stunned but eventually chuckled.

He chuckled too; then, to quench the flame, he swiftly stuffed his blazing right hand into the trouser pocket of his blue overalls, while at the same time whipping a lit cigarette from behind his left ear with his other hand.

The saddler-boys were quite astonished.

Folk who had never seen our Franz walk on his hands through our woodshed, or who had never seen our papier-mâché mermaid; or folk who had not witnessed Franz's shins being tickled by her inky-blue tentacles while swimming with his trouser legs rolled up, did not belong in our Inner Circle of the Initiated.

And that person would certainly not find themselves seated on the Harley Davidson that Franz rolled out of his dimly lit garage and into the bright sun on those beautiful days—so that we, the courageous and fully cocked, might spring ourselves free of Earth's gravity and find ourselves seated on that humungous, cosmic saddle.

They were our great fortune, the red-hot stigmata of joy that seared our calves and ankles when we took the wide curve behind the Wynon cheese factory, until we could no longer bear the centrifugal forces pressing our naked flesh against those fiery exhaust pipes.

Only when we were back home again did fortune transform herself
into pain.

The stigmata seared and stung.

Then someone smeared table butter on them and strictly forbade us to go on any more preposterous rides.

FIVE

Behind his commanding back, the dark vacuum smelled of tangy leather.

Blurs of asphalt and grass shot by my pointy, naked knees.

Manhole covers glimmered.

The thirty-two-year-old clutching the motorbike's handlebars was my father.

The landscape we soared into throbbed like an open cranium.

Its edges were lit up in bright crimson.

A drunken farmer lurched toward us in his decrepit Ford pickup.

Dad whizzed out into the field and stomped on his brakes.

From the open trunk of the farmer's zigzagging pickup, you could see the milk sloshing and splashing.

"A narrow escape," I blurted to Father.

Something about that sentence struck me as wrong when I said it, but I didn't correct myself. He raised me off the seat and pressed me to his chest.

We breathed deep and sat down next to each other in the short grass.

Hydrocephalus.

A bulbous, furry, legless insect, enlarged as a loaded hay truck, shot toward us, slicing a straight line across the countryside.

And then... Again, we hit the hot road.

I tried to imagine my younger brother, whose head, it was said, was growing way too fast. Alarmed by this strange expansion, we rushed further down into the valley.

Frantic and titanic at the same time, its growth far outpaced itself.

And, in the state capital, the lights popped on all at once.

My brother was dozing when we stepped into the whitewashed room, his jellified little head rested on the white pillow and knew nothing of itself.

I, too, didn't see what I knew.

That medical expression "water on the brain" only taught us life's relevance sometime later.

I turned toward Mother's birth-giving bed. She lay in a puddle of pain and searched for me with her hand.

I did not remove my leather cap.

Frustration began to fill the hospital room with electricity.

All eyes lit up green.

The bundle awakened:

"Together, we shall carry you clear across the world," Father said.

And when we arrived home again, the laundry lady was still perched above the ironing board, starching our stiff collars.

SIX

Only when we were sick and during public holidays did we sleep on the second floor. The rest of the time, we settled on the ground level in the bakery, the kitchen, and the shop, and in the small vestibule next door with its frost crystals in the windows.

In the summer, beaming red geraniums healthily caressed our windowsills. These were the labors of Mother's green thumb. These plants represented the other side of her life:

Verdant and rosy and lush.

Whatever Mother laid her hand on took root, flowered, bore fruit, and drove a glimmer into her dull eyes.

That glimmer faded by the time the chrysanthemums were wilting.

The Trading Station was what Father stubbornly insisted on calling our little living room—mostly because of his desk, with the blue cash ledger in the top drawer, and because of the heap of invoices and receipts lying lazily in a pile in the furthest corner.

His desk served as a storage place for clothes, mail, printed matter, accumulated student stuff. Dust collected between erasers, the tweezers Grandmother plucked her beard hairs with, paper clips, and blunt pencils.

We lounged around the pullout table, the threadbare couch, the loudspeakers with the tones of our country's main station, Radio Beromünster, pressed to our ears—so as not to disturb the customers lingering behind the dusty shop door which was continuously left ajar.

From time to time, the powdery flour deliveryman or a chocolate salesman or, occasionally, the egg man, would join us here. Sometimes, Mother would spread out a luxurious, handwoven fabric that had been gifted to us by a well-mannered traveler from northern Switzerland—and then she would come alive.

With her meager saved-up housekeeping money Mother beautified
the house and the Christmas vestibule, year by year—and added
her additional cushions or a chestnut-red tablecloth that matched
the curtains.

Evenings, she handpicked and knotted a particular necktie for Father. It was saturated with pastel colors—not shiny, but dull and comforting.

Unexpected visits were rewarded with mountains of sweet goodies in the Trading Station. Family members and acquaintances dove headfirst into those lumpy candy offerings.

And there was black tea spiked with Spanish wine.

"I'm unable to stomach this mix," Mrs. Brettschneider said, then poured herself a tot straight from the bottle, leaving the tea and sweets to her grandchildren.

She spoke with hands that were tanned from tobacco juice. She was the quickest cigarette roller in the region, and she nattered as she rolled, like a semi-automatic machine gun.

The day Franz swaggered into the room with his new Blaupunkt, the words caught even in Mrs. Brettschneider's well-oiled throat.

Uncle Franz had managed, somehow, to acquire this Cadillac of radios from a bankrupt estate.

He proudly translated the announcement from Radio Luxembourg even before he'd connected the apparatus and plunked it on the table.

We could make out the loudspeakers' vacuum tubes behind its beige cover. The knobs reminded the egg man of Franz's accordion with its weighted ivory keys.

The egg man shot off his mouth, claiming that from now on even folk with stubby fingers could create music. Franz smacked Egg's hands away from the dials, then read us the list of Europe's radio stations as if he had been reciting a poem.

Then he turned with his left hand, looking for the world's wheel.

Not until that moment—with a rapid flick of his wrist, he flipped open the shell of the apparatus—did we realize that in the right-hand corner, a turntable was spinning.

Franz had also brought along a vinyl record.

The word Brunswick was emblazoned on the black disc.

It had to be another word for joy.

The floor wobbled ecstatically.

In an instant, the gruff voice of the trumpet player drove off Mrs. Brettschneider with her three grandchildren, allowing the rest of us to huddle in closer.

On the sunny side of the street …

"Who wants to walk into joy," we heard that grumpy old woman warbling as she waddled away.

Only after sundown did we go back to listening to the news on Beromünster Radio. And when the rest of the houses in the neighborhood had already hung up their socks, we still hung on to the echo of those trusted voices:

Von Theodor H. from London,

Hans O. from Paris,

Heiner G. from New York

Their inflections inspired our imaginings of the immense world, of distant cities and conflicts that molded and deeply stamped our countrified heads.

Franz squeezed his nostrils with thumb and forefinger:

"So I can better hear," he said and then swallowed a pill for wanderlust and pain.

Sol, my little brother, after his long, uneventful mornings, was the first one to lose his heart to the shortwave.

In order to listen to the newest pop hits and that explosive American Rock 'n' Roll and *Krautrock*—for which he practically leaped out of his seat—he was even willing to endure our northern neighbor's vacuum cleaner advertisements.

This all happened long after Grandmother had definitively given up the war with her beard hairs and had become a hearty, church-going supplicant.

SEVEN

After all the birds and the fish, Grandfather decided to move on and cultivate honeybees.

"You'll need your honey too," he told us. "I'll make it for you."

He built himself an insect paradise close to the cemetery and was soon immune to their stings.

He slathered himself in sugar water, swapped out the honeycombs, cleaned out the dead critters from their entrance holes, and greeted the queen regally.

If his bee folk would start swarming, he'd dive into his personal fountain of youth.

He smeared his shaved head with honey and wore the renegades as his gold humming crown when he stumbled home.

"The queen, too, has a stinger but uses it mainly to live or die in a duel with her rival. The drones, on the other hand, are quite defenseless and, when their time has come, are murdered in a bloody drone battle."

Grandfather lectured to our apprentice baker as if he had been preaching to the Levites every spring and fall before he had spun his honey.

Wherever you touched, you stuck.

And, every now and then, a bee found its way into someone's cavernous mouth, and then they were promptly rushed off to the emergency room.

Evenings, that liquid gold dribbled and drizzled into barrels and fermenting cauldrons.

To counter the hard winter (when I first went to school and was finally out in the real world), Grandfather recommended that I eat his honey sandwiches and don his blue military uniform with its fancy silver epaulets.

That abrasive blue cloth was promptly rolled out of Grandfather's moth-eaten haversack. Mr. Brettschneider, the family's token-Austrian tailor, who married himself into our family, and acted as if his name came from noble birth, carefully measured me up.

At the behest of the adults, fancy silver epaulets, shiny buttons, and that large belt buckle with its sharp tongue were to be handed down accordingly.

I stood there, mummified, in the fitting room of Mr. Brettschneider's dingy tailoring workshop. He sat there cross-legged, sneering devilishly at his desk, the worn tape measure dangling around his neck as if he might hang me with it any second.

Mother began to helplessly tug the rough blue cloth draped on her hapless little child-soldier.

Flies whizzed wildly around our blank heads.

"There once was a soldier in Volgograd," sang Mr. Brettschneider, scrutinizing his own handiwork.

Outside, there was a sudden snow squall.

Twilight fell haphazardly over the battlefield.

It became darker and mustier in Mr. Brettschneider's dingy workshop.

And, in my panic, as was the family habit, I stopped breathing for a minute. And, promptly, the imperial maneuvers of my uncle-in-law and his allied Swiss apiarist and master baker tumbled down into the stratospheres.

For the forthcoming winter I had been promised a windbreaker
with large kangaroo pockets.

I drew my breath for the umpteenth time.

Mother hugged me tight.

We never let go of each other again.

EIGHT

"Get up and walk!"

Grandmother shouted at my brother Sol every morning.

She balanced him on her left foot and raised her arthritic hands imploringly toward the ceiling. The eight-o'clock train, which rushed by our house toward the valley, trailing its empty freight cars, made the windowpanes shudder.

She placed brother on the table, somehow straightened his head and, on her command, he shook a little on the living room table. From this effort, the vein in his temple menacingly swelled, and after a while he collapsed back in upon himself.

The early morning news masked the healer's heavy sighs.

Determined to the very end, Grandmother, shortly before Christmas, summoned her brothers and sisters to pray with her.

From within a dark, deep murmuring, in front of our very own eyes, the pasty-faced arrivals from the Lazarus Chapel slowly raised the living room table off the floor.

Brother, as always, remained firmly planted.

We assured our shocked parents (who had just been out of the house for a minute to grab a breath of fresh air during these heavy-hearted days of the year), when they bumped into shrouded figures in black snowshoes in the doorway, that no harm had come to anyone during these unusual experiments.

It was then that Grandmother finally gave up the ghost.

"If it works, it works. If it doesn't work, it can't hurt." Grandmother repeatedly chanted to herself and, for a minute, became her old self again, but then withdrew with God's militia back into the unheated chapel.

Father, steaming with rage, tore one of the outer windows off its casement and tossed it on the rusty railroad tracks.

Mother wept silently.

We rang up the cash register. I was in charge of the copper and nickel coins, and piled the little cent pieces into a crooked tower that rose all the way to the living room ceiling.

Mother took care of the silvers. Father had it easiest: his few notes were quickly counted up.

On the last day of each month, Father prepared the employee payment packets. They were dark yellow and sealed shut. If there was ever too little in the cash register, Mother would supplement these funds with her meager housekeeping savings.

The staff lit up as soon as they knocked on the living room door. They scribbled their signatures meticulously and ceremoniously and, at the same time, somehow, with a flourish.

It was as if they had been piping a cake with hot butter chocolate cream. But the maids were frequently embarrassed. gripping Father's fountain pen in their fingers, and were visibly relieved when this ritual was over.

Father always threw in an extra five-franc piece for measure. That was just his way. Mother attributed it to his sickness.

NINE

Sickness always been front and center in our family. And, after Grandmother trudged barefoot through the snow in a religious fit and was carried out of the house during the first spring storm (she was as delicate and ancient as brittle autumn leaves), my brother Sol was once again the sickest in the house; so sick, in fact, that everyone happily and generously tended to his every whim.

Large and small alike turned to stare at him and quite frequently stumbled on the curb, snagged their hems and skirts on garden fences; or, gawping, bonked their heads on telegraph poles when I was pushing him through the streets in his high-wheeled pram.

At that time there were few television shows—mostly bland, sensationalist journalism—so we supplemented our local programs with live entertainment.

In those moments when inner doubt suddenly transformed into boundless self-confidence, we stridently called out the obvious idiots by their first names; and, with pointed laughter and the front wheels of his buggy raised, we chased them away and avoided their scattered selves long thereafter.

The high point of our unwitting showmanship was surely upstaged
by Father's grand mal seizure on the street curb.

It was a Sunday morning when he was stricken during a stroll through the middle of the village. Good Samaritans emerged from their abodes, as if summoned, and surrounded us in a giant haze of curious bodies.

Sol stood up in the choir's dark, humming shadow and stared on helplessly from his rickety buggy.

With a pale face, I knelt beside our twitching father, and, as well as I could, prayed fervently.

After an eternity, which seemed to have transformed my brother and me into two shriveled little old men, the sun now rested at its great zenith.

A smell of roasted meat hung in the air, and I observed Father slowly regain consciousness.

He nodded, rose slowly, and continued on his stroll almost as if nothing at all had occurred.

Father brushed off his fine threads, blew his nose in his Sunday handkerchief, tugged down his dark blue beret, and focused on a distant point on the horizon.

He reached for my brother's buggy and laid his arm around my shoulders.

Without even a glance back at the disconcerted Sunday crowd, we strode through a black tunnel into the brightest afternoon I'd ever known.

TEN

That evening, though, I was struck with fever.

Weird balls of mercury trickled over the duvet and quickly sneaked between the white sheets as another of those thermometers snapped in damp hands.

Mother hung on in my room for ages searching for those lost silver balls of treasure in my bed and in the nooks and crannies of our hardwood floorboards.

Once she was gone, I slipped off my vinegary socks and returned
to Jack:

> *Frère Jacques, Frère Jacques,*
> *Dormez-vous? Dormez-vous?*

I sang quietly up into the ceiling panels.

We'd learned that French canon in kindergarten and had performed
it with up to three harmonies.

Even back then, I knew precisely who the song was about.

The kindergarten teacher secretly sided with me.

Without her, perhaps Jack would never have awoken in
Brettschneider's dingy tailor shop.

When the mercury column of my thermometer shot up over 39
degrees and I struck up the canon again, Jack pulled back the heavy
curtain on his side of the window and just stood there lingering.

Jack was almost a head taller than I, and wore his hair long and straggly. I was sure he could not hold his own as an angel. After all, he was my elder brother.

"I heard the bells," he sighed simply, perched on the edge of my bed.

He knew I wouldn't sleep through my fever.

I couldn't close my eyes against the inflamed world.

When I went beyond the 39-degree limit, Jack gently stroked my eyelids and stood by on command.

I found complete tranquility on the spot and improved in a flash.

That very morning after Jack's last call of duty at my bedside, a moped stood at our front door.

I stroked its silver cylinders and then push-started the machine at a walking pace.

With the cargo trailer behind me loaded with bread, and barely a day fever-free, I swung myself over the seat and already, after the first couple of meters, left Mother's objections behind in the wind.

ELEVEN

I delivered twelve lightly baked French baguettes to the old people's home and their faulty teeth.

In the corridor with its deathbeds at the ready, I held my breath in order not to get infected.

Wet plaster dripped from the ceiling.

I galloped back out of the nursing home hanging onto the trainee cook's apron strings.

Awestruck, he admired my new moped.

Then, as the crow flies, I rushed on to the delivery entrances of the taverns. Even though I was now motorized and no longer arrived with my usual flushed-red face, the waitresses treated me to a large glass of fizzy soda pop, which invigorated me for the rest of my route.

I pissed in a high arch on the tall, golden garden gate of the villa of the local gods, Nägel and Stahl, before I delivered their muesli bread.

An empty trailer improved my aerodynamics.

Hunkered down between handlebar cables, I rocketed down-valley and, more intrepid than ever, screeched on the brakes right next to a very pretty girl.

In those days, no one wore a helmet.

I took the sharp curve, scraped the asphalt with the pedal so that sparks flew, and rammed my shoulder into a flagpole. The loose, wiry cable tore a bloody split over the top of my skull.

Father assisted steadfastly with the shaving and sewing and didn't faint at the doctor's feet until the eighteenth stitch, by which time it was nearly all over.

We both stumbled out of the emergency room, each of us wearing a white turban.

Thankfully, my moped was no worse for wear.

TWELVE

A couple of months after his birth, in order to constrict the rapid growth of his skull, they countersunk two holes in the back of Sol's head. In that countersunk light, you could see a heart thumping beneath his sparse, fuzzy hair.

With a short arm, Sol touched the top of his head, laid his finger on the throbbing spot, and sniggered when I called him "Two-Stroke."

In this fashion each of us had an auxiliary engine.

These contraptions kept us alive.

In the shade of the rubber trees, the gardener's daughter patiently waited for her Zopf bread. I slipped into the greenhouse from behind and surprised her with my bandaged head. We swapped our middle-class woes and then fell silent, tongue entwined, until the glass around us steamed up.

It smelled of damp turf.

The *Hometown Bells* radio show from the gardener's wireless called us back home. It was Saturday evening. The middle class were to be lathered and bathed, and there was a radio play on the evening program.

For a while I called myself Paul Cox, like that wily shark in those radio murder mysteries.

And then, suddenly, the names of the broadcasters changed more frequently, like those of the foreign correspondents whom I had long considered to be irreplaceable and implacable. Not even Viktor W. in Rome, the eternal city, held on.

Despite that, we still remained true to our invisible, ethereal creatures and perched at the living room table Sunday after Sunday, all the way through the evening news.

By the time the national anthem was fading out in the kitchen, Mother would be pulling steaming egg noodles out of the water (which she seasoned only with a splash of Maggi sauce), and we would luxuriate in our midnight feast like little kings—just without our meat and servants.

That weekly late-night meal was a part of an unspoken bond within our family. During that time, Sol would stir from a waking sleep on his upper floor.

I would slurp wine from Father's cloudy glass.

Before we went to bed, we all stepped up to the window together. If I was lucky, Sputnik would sweep through the sky with its monkey. It was certain that the warning lights of the nearby broadcast tower would be flashing in the southern sky. It seemed as if we were gazing at an enormous constellation. As always, during the winter months, Father scanned the skies for Ursa Major toward Orion.

And Mother took a whiff of her sprig of wild lavender.

THIRTEEN

That day, we strolled into the Trading Station and our eyes fell upon an oil painting of a large, naked man leaning next to the living room door. This was surely Father's boldest acquisition in years: art for bread.

He admired that painter, a gentleman of his own generation who strode into the bakery in stained trousers with a rainbow under his fingernails and who always pointed to the darkest loaves of bread.

In one hand, the widest brush, in the other, a rag which simultaneously serves as a loincloth, the painter stands across from his own reflection. The summer heat turns his studio in the hayloft a light amber, just as it does in our painting.

Gary Cooper has almost that same square stance while waiting for the high noon train in Hadleyville's hot village square. The only difference is, he's actually wearing cowboy duds and a sheriff's star: ready and alone, but without any real mandate. That's just the way things go.

We watched that movie on a Sunday afternoon. And after the shoot-out between Kane and Frank Miller we were struck wordless; we were dusty-eyed on the way home and rolled our hips through a desert wasteland.

It was the same way Father had once rolled his hips, after that eternity, when he raised himself back up from the earth, we too strode home through a murky tunnel welling into the light.

At home, Father began the dough fermentation.

Mother combed ricochet shots from my hair.

The painter's feet, even though they can't quite be seen, are firmly planted. He's a reliable man who presents himself as considerate and curious. He has a little mouth under his small mustache.

With critical eyes narrow as slits, our painter must have stepped out of his painting to survey his canvas a hundred times; and with his outstretched hand, he surely carefully measured himself up and painted.

"People should be able to remain firmly planted like that," Father said, removing the nail from his mouth and hammering it into the wall to hang up the painting.

This time he would not stand for any contradiction.

For me, it was all about how the colors had been generously applied.

For you, it was your daily bread.

Father was in complete and utter agreement.

FOURTEEN

When I couldn't sleep after those events in the Wild West, I took the precaution of enquiring about Lot's wife in order to prepare myself, should the subject come up in discussion during Sunday school.

I just couldn't understand why God had set the destruction of Sodom and Gomorrah in motion so mercilessly. He hadn't even spared the children. Above all, I couldn't understand why he had let Lot's wife turn into a pillar of salt.

All she had done was glance back.

"Why does God do things like that to mankind if he loves them?"

Even though he was dead tired, it was a question that Father once again raised.

"That's just the way it goes," he said.

"Since year one, the most heartless, ignorant individuals, the hypocrites and the bootlickers, the truly inhuman, and those who were reckless, who didn't take notice of what was going on behind their backs and hadn't the courage to turn around, were the ones that survived and even emerged unscathed. To them, every catastrophe was fine as long as they were spared the gory details.

"Kudos to Lot's wife," he said, and began pacing restlessly back and forth in the small room, breathing rapidly. Mother started worrying about him.

"Tell your teachers, tell your teacher, that one should praise that woman even though she's not even once allowed to claim her own name in the holy book.

"Tell them that Lot's wife was the only one who turned back despite the dark threat when she heard what was going on behind her.

"When she heard the thunder and the screams and the flashes of those fleeing shadows who bolted and threw themselves at her feet.

"When she felt the heat of a fire that raged at her back."

"Tell your teacher that Lot's wife was the only one to face the fleeing mob with their horrified faces and their eyes glazed over in fear, facing so much ferocity and rage.

"And tell your catechist that we saw Gary Cooper striding alone across the village square in Hadleysville.

"And that he hangs naked on our wall in the living room.

"Tell her that.

"And now, sleep, young man!"

FIFTEEN

Why it was that Sonja married the cattle dealer, of all people (she successfully completed an apprenticeship in his farmyard after graduation), always remained a complete mystery.

The widower had only just come to terms with the death of his first wife, who had passed from thrombosis during childbirth, when we heard rumors of Sonja's upcoming marriage.

Straight through our meager flurries of wedding rice, striding past a row of black umbrellas, the cattle dealer set out with his young bride into a blizzard.

"It's not a good omen," Mother said, "that Sonja married that man today of all days, on Franz's death day."

And we saw her then, too, after that rushed alliance, when the whispers subsided, more and more frequently in our mind's luminous eyes, standing atop her feeding silos in far eastern Switzerland.

Terribly young, beset with a longing for home, and feeling wistful, quite unlike she was in her childhood, she must have been staring in the direction of the Jura mountains, her slow-moving eyes probing the curve of those ancient hills, imagining far more than she could actually see.

For years she kept vigil as the cattle dealer's children stoically outgrew her, until one evening she threw herself headlong into oncoming traffic after letting all the barn animals loose.

From that moment on, even though he never rode them himself, the cattle dealer became even more impassioned about his racing horses. Shortly thereafter, he withered, frail and thin, and fell into a deep depression. Later, it was as if he had been kicked in the head by one of his own draft animals.

He went quite daft.

In a back corner of her sewing room, Sonja left his adolescent children a wooden box with a metal grille.

It was heavy with grey cocoons.

That was a blank November.

Four months later the butterflies emerged:

Blackleg tortoiseshells.

Swallowtails.

There wasn't a single mourning cloak among them.

SIXTEEN

Five years prior to Sonja's wedding, news had reached us up at the Trading Station that Franz, Father's Alaska-émigré brother, had died in a plane crash in the woods near our home.

Franz had worn many hats:

He played the accordion with nine fingers, recited poetry, and often had a headache.

And he had magic fingers, could ride heavy motorcycles, and fly.

From the day of his death, we never tore that page from the calendar.

Newspapers announced that a single-engine airplane, CAP 10 B, had crashed close to T. in the forest. Franz and his lady companion from Fort Yukon died on the spot.

It was also said the airplane had been stolen twenty minutes before the crash and that the takeoff had been entirely reckless.

The plane had flown directly to T. where it circled over the aviator's own hometown, throttling and sporadically dropping.

"After a failed attempt to turn a sharp left turn to gain height, the pilot could not avoid a collision with the looming trees," three forest rangers noted.

Eyewitnesses who had observed the flight maneuver even pointed out to the investigative commission that the guilty pilot, while madly circling his own neighborhood, had not paid primary attention to the flying of the craft itself.

Franz was buried in the south end of the cemetery. His girlfriend's ashes were shipped back to Alaska.

Father did not take possession of Franz's inheritance. An anemic court official rolled the old Harley out of the woodshed in lieu of a downpayment for the junked aircraft.

The day after, Father claimed he heard soft accordion tones while standing over Franz's grave. It seemed to him as if that instrument had secreted itself below the earth to keep Franz company.

On the 8th of May 1945, a day that was unforgettable to all who were at the Blue Elephant, Franz had been playing at a dance until the early hours of the morning.

Shortly before daybreak, with the help of some military-band musicians and hard-drinking airmen, a black accordion case was raised onto the window ledge in one of the guest rooms on the third floor of the inn. In order to heighten the explosive effect of the peace bomb, the accordionist was urged to fill the bellows with water.

With much celebratory participation from the whole peace brigade, the oozing instrument burst with a dull, sloppy thud on the village square next to the pharmacy.

Throughout the course of daybreak, hardly a home in the area didn't acquire an ivory relic, or at least a damp splinter of wood, in memory of that peace accord.

Sonja's father unfolded his checkered handkerchief on Franz's grave. The letters "O. WOE" were embroidered on that piece of cloth, which was the size of a parachute.

He'd previously blown his nose on it.

Above, the grey aircraft of the Government Topography Office circled the mourners.

SEVENTEEN

On his twentieth birthday, Franz had hiked home over the Saint Gotthard Pass from his intermittent familial banishment only to emigrate, for the first time, to Alaska. There, he spat ice cubes, and his tremendous jet of urine shattered on the frozen earth; there, he shared his catfish with two Inuit women.

It was on the shores of the Yukon River that, after a hunting expedition, he lay with a smashed foot and was subsequently dragged through the snow and ice back to the camp by a grizzly.

Franz had often recounted these and other events in our Trading Station after his temporary return from the icy deserts of Alaska. At the prompting of his spellbound audience, he repeatedly brought these tales alive again—that was, after Grandfather's anger toward his wayward son had finally subsided, and the men listening urgently needed a heartwarming glass of schnapps.

So as not to leave me in the dark, it was Franz who had also first nicknamed my younger brother Sol.

On the day Franz died, I left the narrow room, sat cross-legged under the Black Forest grandfather clock at the end of the corridor, and weighed the two iron pinecone counterweights in my hands. The clock had stopped.

I wanted to toss those heavy pull-weights through the veranda window down onto the railroad tracks to finally balance accounts with time. Then, I suddenly felt the residual heat from the bread oven through the floorboards rise within me. It made my sadness about Franz seem bearable.

I let the weights sink down again.

After Franz passed on, Father didn't have a brother to take care of him anymore, or whom he could keep an eye on. He only had us left, his stand-in soldiers who stood epileptically in a circle, impatiently and palely waiting for his return when he had another one of his episodes.

We turned Sol to the wall so he didn't have to face the fact.

Sometimes, Father was already chuckling again when he raised himself up. He acted as if nothing at all had happened—or, occasionally, he hissed like a wounded creature.

In the nights that followed, when I couldn't hear him snoring through the wall, I sneaked into my parents' room to press my ear against his mouth and make sure he was still breathing.

Mother, who stirred awake, took me by the hand and slid me through the Christmas room to Father's books and our black piano, past the grey cloud formations of our upholstered furniture, and back to bed.

In the light of the dim moon illuminating her white nightdress, I fell asleep again.

EIGHTEEN

We found things most difficult in times of relative painlessness. We couldn't bear the latency of new wounds and turned ourselves to a foreign suffering that we only managed to tolerate as badly as our own woes.

That's why, for safety's sake, we cut our fingers, poured boiling water on our thighs, broke our collarbone or a rib. We sacrificed this period of non-suffering in order to appease it with skirmishes before something more serious occurred—and also, when Mother, pale and pinch-lipped, her hair gone chalk white, came out of a clinic that had been recommended to us in good faith by its clientele to counter her growing depression.

She put up a weak resistance when Father and I delivered her to the sanatorium.

"Let's go," was all she said when, a few weeks later, we loaded her suitcases back into the car. She didn't throw a single glance back at that stork of an orderly who stood there in the doorway of the institution to see her off.

The first thing she did back home was make that heating pad she warmed her cold bed with disappear. And she was vehemently opposed to us buying a newer, better one.

She was fearful of the electrical currents.

If you follow the line of her roses, you'll reach the southern point of the small garden where, with Grandfather, I planted two trees together: a cottonwood tree for Sol's birth and, somewhat later, a stately linden for myself.

We barely talked to each other, just dug up dirt, rammed in supporting poles, tightened support strings, and schlepped water back and forth.

Three decades later, the future owner would cut down the cottonwood, possibly due to pressure from the Swiss Railways (our Orient Express, which shot straight past our garden fence).

They had been eyeing that steep but profitable stretch since their early pioneering days.

The felling of that tree must have coincided precisely with my brother Sol's death.

We had a sun chiseled onto his gravestone and left enough space for our parents' names. A few years later, they nestled in, right there beside him.

On a starry January night, I placed them on the belt of Orion, Father's favorite constellation in the winter sky. With Sol wedged between them, they dangle their legs in the universe, afraid of nothing.

Because he slept in the darkness, I couldn't really place Jack anywhere.

NINETEEN

My linden tree still stands there today. Its massive branches reach under the overhead line that has become quite useless, the railway track now totally disused.

Cattails grow between the ties. There's no luster on the tracks, no linesman with his short steps and a red warning flag in his quiver, and no one to hand him a cream tart through the kitchen window.

With his worn-out teeth, he used to bite down so hard into the pastry that the custard quite frequently splashed on his brown brogues.

That man from the railway and we, his negligible catering staff, on the edge of that steep stretch.

On afternoons off from school, I carried our family's heavy Sol up the virtually unscalable steps into a section of the third-class cabins.

My brother would sit upright next to me on the wooden bench and from under his heavily loaded forehead stare out into the landscape rushing by.

Traveling made us feather light.

We couldn't forget he was unable to walk. But driving, flying, singing, we knew would work.

We outfoxed that everyday force of gravity and rode the well-monitored railway stretch, smiling triumphantly past our parental home.

The light in our section turned pine green, and we rattled into the ravine. In three national languages my brother read the warning sign that forbade us to throw solid objects out the window. A pair of these enameled placards was fixed to every wooden cornice.

It was then time to toss those empty bottles I had smuggled along in my blue duffel bag out the window and into the creek.

I hit the rock dead on.

Ecstatic, Sol excitedly slapped both his hands on his thighs. It tingled in the back of his neck from all the laughing and he began to hyperventilate. I covered his mouth and nose until he snorted and could breathe again.

On this stretch, we also envisioned our failed common dreams.

We had dumped the largest pile of stones onto the railway tracks, ground the phosphorus from a whole pack of matches into a plastic bag; or even more impressively, set carbide charges on this stretch of track, in order to finally derail that merciless, thundering train.

Nothing ever happened that could derail our day out, though; that is not until, after a massive outburst that stunned us, the young neighbor woman who lived above the kiosk near the station broke into wild, contorted screams of childbirth.

From her balcony, perched on the handrail, she frantically shouted down at us. In any case, no one had the right to get this beautiful woman pregnant, least of all the accountant.

She gave him twins.

Our treasure must still be buried between the rail and the tree. The piece of stovepipe we hid it in will have rusted away by now.

Didn't we sign it in our own blood?

And how did the words of our pledge and promise go? I can't quite remember.

Back then, we must have felt that neither the Rome nor the London route, nor the Paris nor the Beinwil-Beromünster stretch, would have ever sufficed.

It was only within or under the earth we could go on.

We visualized nothing less than an eternity, painted a knight's helmet on our coat of arms in reverence to our most noble ancestors or perhaps subconsciously as a symbol of the passing of time.

And because it was precious, to us we rested that roebuck antler right next to it.

Adventurers, explorers, and world voyagers, perhaps some kind of freedom fighters is what we yearned to be: Sonja, Sonja's brothers, my own backward-parked brother and me.

Despite all that, we still managed to get the train driver to slip his foot off the dead man's pedal, to pull the whistle murderously and curse when, in our life-or-death courage, we squeezed our faces into the rails until we felt the Orient Express in our innards.

It was kind of like a wild scream of childbirth.

TWENTY

Back over the shoulder, a glance falls upon the covered terrace with its asphalt floor. Sol sits on his oversized three-wheeler and makes his rounds under my custody. I urge him on. Smoke rises from the brick chimney of the laundry room; the slapping of fresh sheets sounds like the ragged scraps of an Italian folk song.

Next to our house, the Orient Express's semaphore signal falls back into starting position. The hoisted railway crossing gates point straight up into the cloud formation again.

On the morning of my thirteenth birthday, a fellow student painted
a full moon on the grey schoolhouse ceiling.

"Your brother's head, a watermelon!"

I just stood there, blinded by all their laughter.

In the afternoon the smoke from our chimney swirled down onto the covered terrace.

"Let it rip!" I roared.

My brother took my orders seriously, pushed off, calculated the curve too tightly, and crashed onto the tarmac. He didn't scream, because, as usual, the air was knocked out of him. I felt the fury of my pent-up anger, but was relieved when it smashed against my red inner walls, then fell to my knees and pushed air through the casualty's nose into his lungs, pressing a handkerchief against his temples. He was now balled together and shaking from the bewildering pain.

Our stressed parents carried my unconscious brother into the house, pulled the Christmas curtain in front of me, and shut out the world.

As if hard work didn't bother her in the slightest, Marietta stood on the bridge of the ocean liner and waved a white kerchief back and forth like the other folk standing there.

I had sought protection under her ample wings.

Twelve years after the war, Marietta had come to us from her southern homeland to buy herself a new eye. Her beauty beguiled whoever stood to her right. If you switched sides though, you stood aghast by the devastation of her young, left face. Shortly before the end of the war, a frightened soldier had shot out one of her eyes. Since then, her face had been divided into a handicapped Catholic side and a proud Latin one.

During May devotions, despite being a Protestant, I was occasionally permitted to accompany Marietta. Mostly, she also kept her healthy eye closed, and I worshipped her unashamedly. When my parents weren't home, I'd confide my secrets to her, my head lazing in her lap.

"Alfa," I whispered, when she called me her "Romeo mio."

My mother's relationship with her southern employee was as divided as Marietta's young face. Mother utterly trusted Marietta's damaged side; she should have loved to lay her hand on it daily to help it heal or at least to comfort the girl. On the other hand, the beguiling part of her face gave Mother the willies. Mother was not that old herself, and she deeply loathed, as she frequently and decisively concluded, this one-sided courtship display that had the entire male workforce turning their cat-calling heads.

Mother was concerned about my innocence, of course.

Once, she stumbled upon us as I lay on the floor of Marietta's little attic apartment, pretending to be a big bad wolf. I had just eaten a piece of chalk, and the squeaking of my freshly broken voice alarmed her. Mother stood in the doorway while Marietta, forgetting herself, surgically extracted seven young goats from my shorts.

I never experienced a fairy tale that deeply ever again—and, of course, I reached the conclusion that true happiness is wordless and only lasts a short spell. I was convinced of this from that afternoon on.

Later, upon her request, week after week, I shaved Marietta's armpits and lathered up her tender calves. She had discovered America for both of us. It was probably wrong of me, of all people, to have stopped her from dyeing her black hair blonde.

Over the shop counter, a customer translated the letter from Sicily a stunned Marietta handed to us:

I have found a man who lives on the outskirts of Agrigento who would likely accept Marietta even with her damaged eye. You should therefore save the additional expenses and let her carry the whole seven-month earnings home in her purse.

Marietta departed.

Only her damaged eye remained dry.

When my photos of Marietta's departure were developed, I asked the photographer (who, from beneath his black blanket, had captured my brother and me like two angels), to transform the picture into one that Marietta had not left behind—namely, to flip the picture horizontally and to retouch it with a healthy eye. With watered-down ink and his finest badger-hair paintbrush, he managed to spirit away the piercing pain in Marietta's face forever.

I kept that picture for myself.

TWENTY-ONE

Whoever wants to walk into joy,
Knows Dill's has the finest threads
For every dapper man or boy.

With this rhyme, the new tailor in town took his revenge on Brettschneider, who, after the ensuing competitive pressure, immediately withdrew with his wife into the Austrian Vorarlberg. That was fine by me. Naturally, I knew that with this slogan, the successful shopkeeper had not only driven off Brettschneider but also shamelessly appropriated from the poet Emanuel Geibel (1815–1884).

In Regli's class we had learned all the Geibel poems in the blue songbook by heart. During that time, Regli had been our teacher; yet still, even into his later retirement, he wanted to gift us something more permanent. He also taught us the melodies, even though he was really just a German teacher and almost always sang flat.

Regli was also the fellow who promised me a new shock absorber and kept that promise. During a hot and heavy summer afternoon just before a downpour, I had given him a ride on my moped's carrier rack all the way out to the old people's home.

I'd just returned back to the village from a big tour and was lounging around the station when Regli limped out of the train. I casually offered him a ride.

Since Father's forty-fifth birthday there has been no bread to be delivered. He'd gone from being a "Crumbler" to a "Voltman." He wandered through households with his sharp pencil, precisely noting people's electricity and water usage in his little black book.

To rid himself finally of that illness-inducing night work, he abandoned his "daily bread," as he called it, and became "a door-to-door" fellow.

A straightforward manner, he maintained, despite the irritation he could see in the eyes of his electricity users, allowed him—between the small irreverence of his new and extensive circle of customers—to find a middle way and, within that, to survive and remain a somewhat intact human being.

After a while, even his superior, a cadaverous technocrat and stickler from the lower village, began coming down off his high horse and started to see matters with revitalized eyes and a renewed respect.

In his jacket pockets, filled with dog biscuits, erasers, cigarettes, his medical emergency kit, and spare pencils, Father always carried a flashlight. A headlamp would have probably been more practical for navigating damp spaces beneath floorboards, stairwells, and basements, spiderweb-shrouded attic corners and foul toilets, in order to reach that black electric box with its counter-dial.

Quite possibly, for our sakes, Father wanted to shelter us from ridicule and thus forwent mounting a Cyclops's eye.

TWENTY-TWO

Roughly and boorishly, with steel forceps, the doctor manhandled Mother's private parts and snapped the healthy boy's neck at birth.

Father never hesitated to come to the point when I walked with him through the suburbs. It had become increasingly difficult to park my moped and amble through the remote courtyards with their chained dogs and cesspools; but here we were, and I listened and asked questions.

Before Father answered me, he picked up a pebble and made as if to toss it at the rough skull of the early-rising moon—he pointed out how damp the local wheat was now; and how, despite the remonstrations of the local farmers, without mixing in foreign imports, you could no longer bake a decent loaf of bread.

With an outstretched arm he pointed over the land.

On the edge of the field stood an abandoned transformer station with a little baroque tower and a red-tile roof.

Rapunzel, Rapunzel!

He had often called up to the tower—long before he ever had anything to do with electricity.

Rapunzel, Rapunzel,
Let down your hair!

He would never have to wait very long until the window under the rusty eaves opened wide and my mother's beautiful face appeared within that weathered frame.

On Ascension Day, as the procession passed with its sluggish prayers and shying horses, gaily-colored canopies and potbellied priests, Mother and Father had discovered the tower key hidden in the high grass.

They had climbed the iron stairs past the insulators, past the transformers and Y-connectors, and stepped into the narrow tower chamber.

And together, in the breaking dawn, they began to supply the entire village with electricity.

"As a visible expression of our love, shortly thereafter, a light burned in every house in the village," Father said.

For a few moments, Father's words illuminated that young couple in my head in a way I could never have imagined my schoolmates' parents.

Quickly thereafter, somewhat embarrassed, Father wiped that fleeting image from my forehead and returned to the inexorable darkening of Mother's soul—whose battle with the angels had probably long been lost, even before Jack's birth.

"Quite possibly, she had already given up when we last returned from the electric tower," Father said, "when her pregnancy was certain."

In my memory, Jack's crucifix still leans against that man-high pyre in the woodshed, in the same spot where it was deposited.

Should anyone ever stumble across that crossbeam with the ten
letters ...

It belongs to me.

FIN

Klaus Merz was born in 1945 in Aarau and lives in Unterkulm, Switzerland. He has won many literary awards, including the Hermann Hesse Prize for Literature, the Swiss Schiller Foundation Poetry Prize and the Friedrich Hölderlin Prize in 2012. He has published over 40 works of poetry and fiction. His latest novel is *The Argentinian* (*Der Argentinier*, Haymon, 2009) and his recent collections of verse are *Unexpected Development* (*Unerwarteter Verlauf*, Haymon, 2013), *Helios Hauls* (*Helios Transport*, Haymon 2016), *firm* (*firma*, Haymon 2019) and *In the House, Still Light* (*Noch Licht im Haus*, Haymon, 2023). In 2024 Klaus Merz won the Grand Prix for Swiss Literature (Switzerland's highest literary prize).

Marc Vincenz is a multi-lingual translator, poet, fiction writer, journalist, editor, musician and artist. He has published over 40 books of poetry, fiction and translation. His recent poetry collections, include, *The Pearl Diver of Irunmani, A Splash of Cave Paint, The King of Prussia is Drunk on Stars, The Mayfly Codex,* IRØNCLAD, and forthcoming in 2026 with White Pine Press, *No More Animal Poems.* His translation of award-winning Swiss poet and novelist, Klaus Merz' selected poems, *An Audible Blue,* won the 2023 Massachusetts Book Award for Translated Literature. He translates from the German, Romanian, French, Icelandic, and Spanish.